A Wolf's Tail

10 Little Rabbits

Ten little rabbits hop out to dine.
But are they alone?

Fold along the dotted line ▶

Cut along dashed line ✂

Little Nipper Press

Ten little rabbits hopped out to dine;
One got caught in a net and then there were nine.

Two little rabbits left. Now we're nearly done;
One became a rabbit pie and then there was . . .

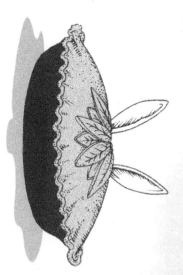

One little rabbit all by himself;
Went to the library and chose a book from the shelf . . .

WOLVES

POST CARD

THIS SPACE MAY BE USED FOR
PRINTED OR WRITTEN MATTER

For
Oleander Grrrabbit
(because I love you)
and the pottery pals
(because I promised)
X X X

Text and illustrations copyright © Emily Gravett 2005, 2015
Moral rights asserted. Printed in China

A CIP catalogue record for this book is available from the British Library.

First published 2005 by

MACMILLAN
Children's Books

Published in 2006 by Macmillan Children's Books
This edition published 2015
by Macmillan Children's Books
an imprint of Pan Macmillan
a division of Macmillan Publishers International Ltd
20 New Wharf Road, London N1 9RR
Associated companies throughout the world
www.panmacmillan.com

ISBN: 978-1-4472-9970-7

1 3 5 7 9 8 6 4 2

www.emilygravett.com

Rabbit went to the library.
He chose a book about . . .

03/07/1991		
12/06/1992	26/04/1997	
02/10/1992		09/03/2002
07/12/1993	07/10/1997	
29/05/1994		08/05/2002
17/06/1995	14/02/1998	10/05/2003
20/06/1995		17/03/2004
20/11/1996	28/07/1998	04/04/2004
14/02/1997	22/09/2000	12/02/2005
		09/08/2005
		24/09/2005

GREY WOLVES live in packs of
between two and ten animals.

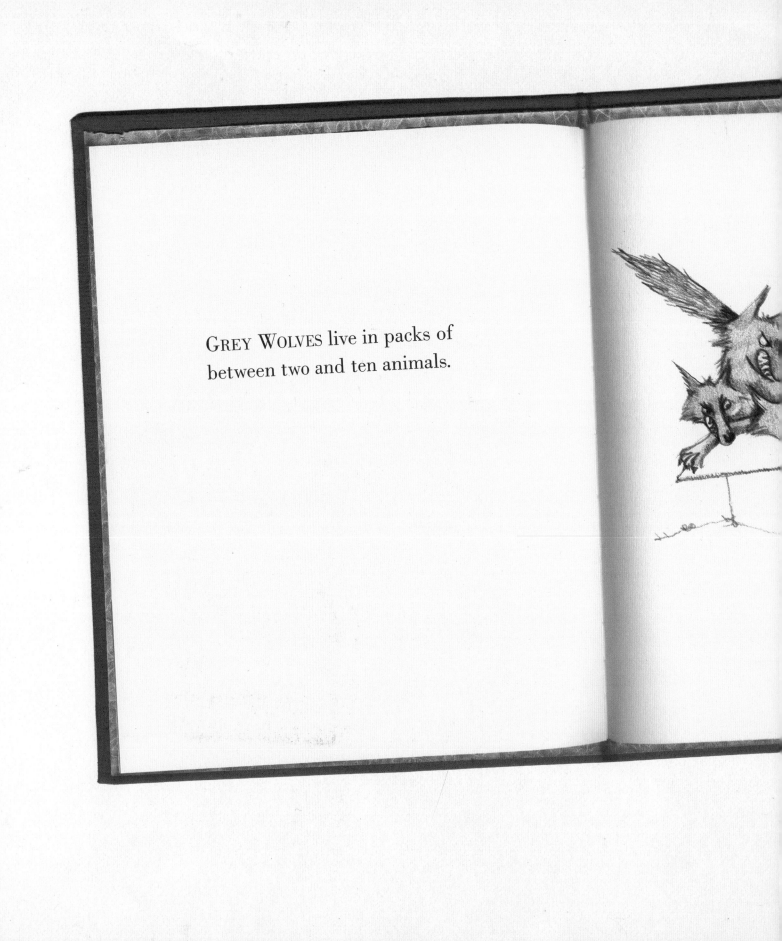

They can survive almost anywhere:
from the Arctic Circle . . .

. . . to the outskirts of towns and villages.

In some areas wolves have retreated
to places where fewer people live,
such as forests and woodland.

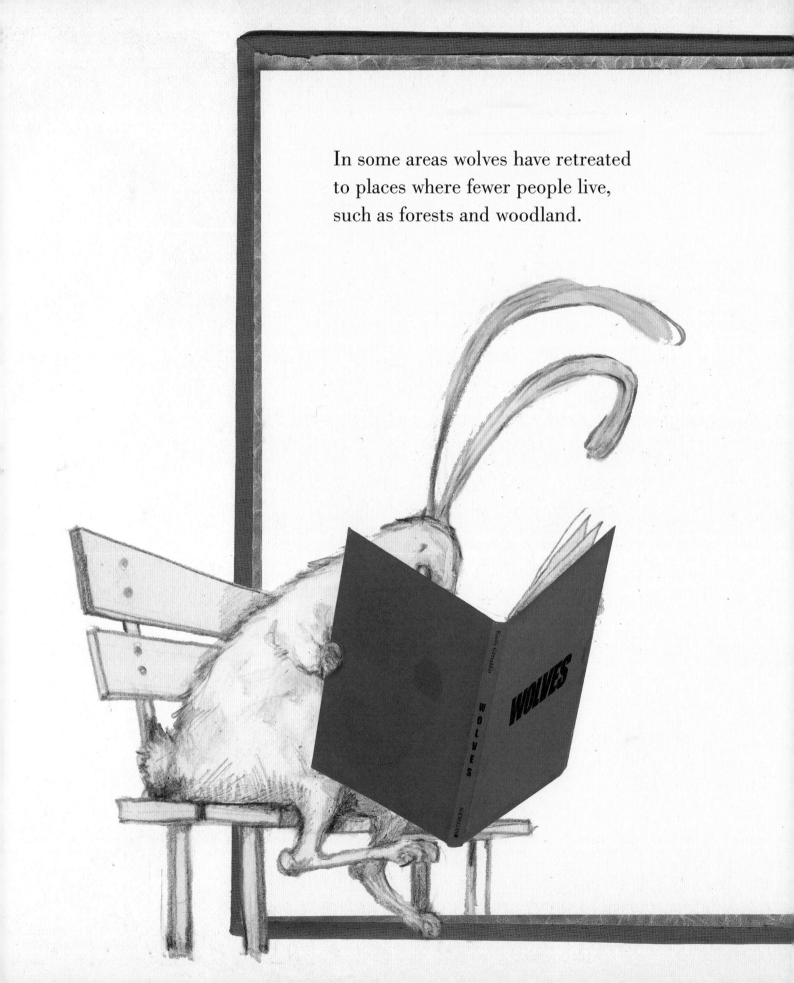

They have sharp claws . . .

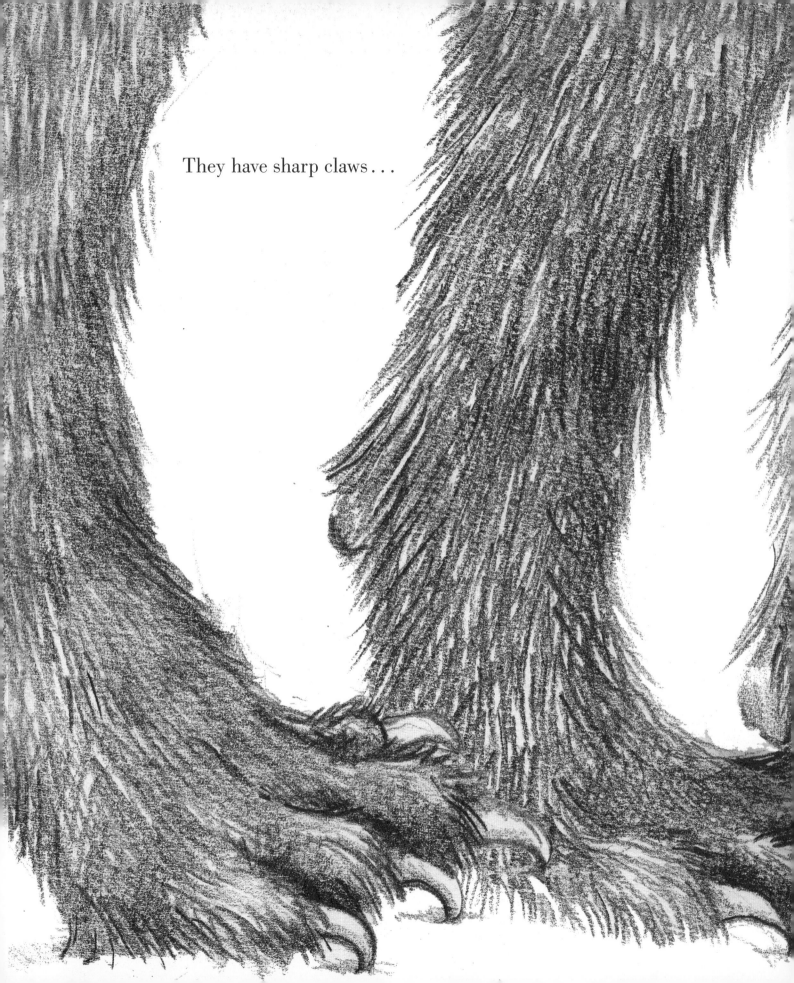

. . . bushy tails . . .

. . . and dense fur, which harbours fleas and ticks.

An adult wolf has 42 teeth.
Its jaws are twice as powerful
as those of a large dog.

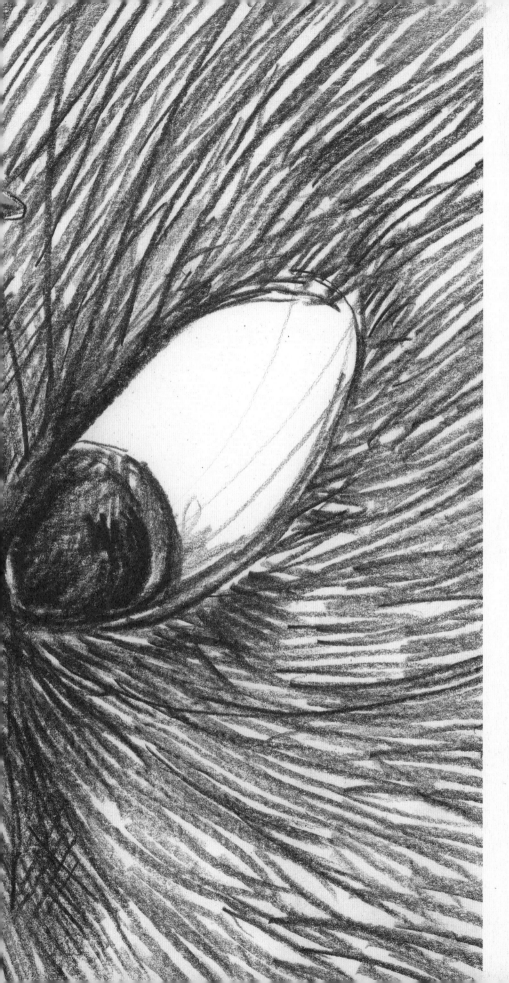

Wolves eat mainly
meat. They hunt
large prey such
as deer, bison and
moose.

They also enjoy
smaller mammals,
like beavers, voles
and . . .

. . . rabbits.

The author would like to point out
that no rabbits were eaten during
the making of this book.
It is a work of fiction.
And so, for more sensitive readers,
here is an alternative ending.

Luckily this wolf was a vegetarian, so they
shared a jam sandwich, became the best of
friends, and lived happily ever after.

If undelivered please return to
West Bucks Public Burrowing Library
36 Warren Wood
Nibbleswick

Burrow more books

Burrowed Wok

Carrotenese

Take Away

43 RABBIT RUN · THE HUTCH
DITCHLING ROAD · SALAD PATCHAM
TELEPHONE ORDERS WELCOME

TELEPHONE 260497

DELIVERY SERVICE AVAILABLE
7 EVENINGS A WEEK

From: 5.30pm – 11.00pm

Within 3 Miles £1.00, 4-5 Miles £1.50

FREE Lawn Crackers
on orders over £10

FREE Morning Dew
on orders over £30

· OPENING HOURS ·
Monday - Thursday   5pm - 11.30pm
Friday - Saturday   5pm - 12 Midnight
Sunday   5pm - 11.00pm

RABBIT MAIL
POSTAGE PAID
HQ 6733
GREAT BURROW

Angora Organics
GARDENING CATALOGUE
Every seed you need for the perfect patch.

G. RABBIT
LANE'S END BURROW
THE LONG FIELD
NIBBLESWICK

Nine little rabbits looked up and saw the weight;

One was looking at the ground and then there were eight.

Eight little rabbits think their burrow's heaven;

One went outside alone and then there were seven.

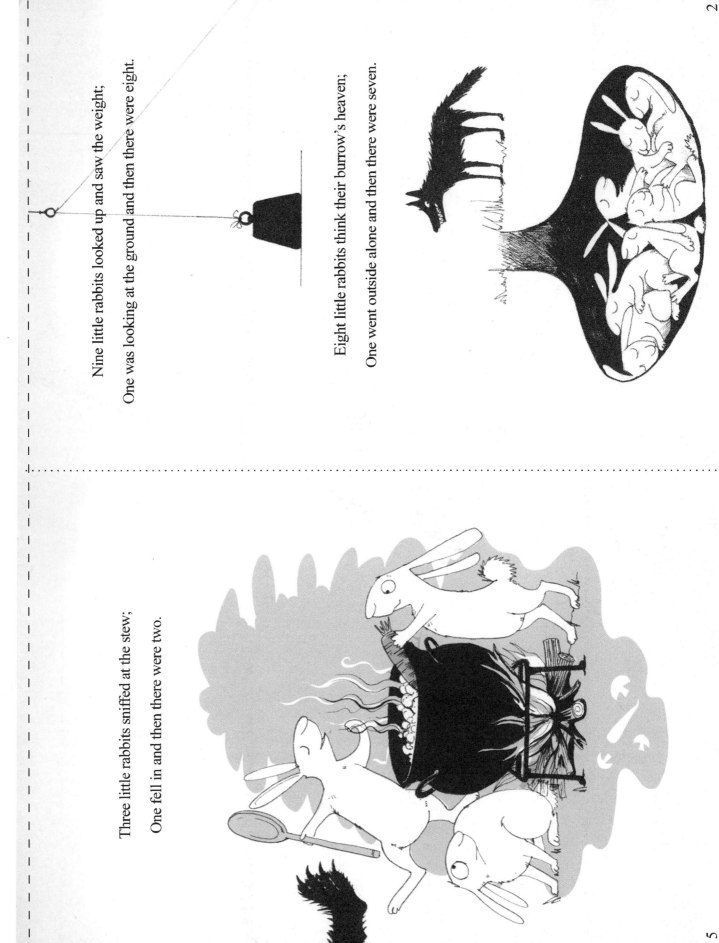

Three little rabbits sniffed at the stew;

One fell in and then there were two.

Cut along here ✂

fold dotted line

Seven little rabbits gnawing on sticks;

One turned out to be a snake and then there were six.

Six little rabbits spied honey in a hive;

One went in to get some and then there were five.

Five little rabbits, each with a lucky paw;

One was *not* so lucky and then there were four.

Four little rabbits hid behind a tree;

A wolf was on the other side and then there were three.